PUMPKINHEAD

ERIC ROHMANN

ALFRED A. KNOPF ✺ NEW YORK

OTHO was born
with a pumpkin
for a head.

And despite what one might think, he was not seen as a curiosity by his family.

One day Otho was outside tossing a ball. High above, a black bat saw a flash of orange in the yards below. Tired of cold, damp caves, he thought Otho's head would make a fine place to live. The bat said, "I can nest in it, feed in it; there's meat and rind and seed in it!"

The black bat dropped from the sky and flew off with Otho's pumpkin head in its claws. Helpless, Otho watched his body running this way and that, growing ever smaller as they flew higher and higher.

Otho was a healthy lad with a large and solid head. Otho's head grew heavier and heavier with every wing beat, and the bat sighed, "Your head would make a perfect home, but I am weary to the bone, and since it's heavy as a stone and I can't carry it alone, so long."

Otho squeezed shut his eyes, prepared for the worst, but much to his surprise he splashed instead of splatted . . . and floated on the sea.

Days and nights, through calm and storm, Otho drifted.

Until one day a great and ravenous fish swallowed him whole.

Then later, an even greater and even more ravenous squid grabbed the fish and squeezed. Otho shot out like a cork from a popgun.

When he finally had the courage to open his eyes, Otho was drifting again—but trouble was looming.

A fisherman caught Otho in his net and dragged him aboard. He said, "I've seen lionfish, zebrafish, hogfish, monkfish, angelfish, devilfish, catfish, dogfish, goatfish, redfish, knifefish, clownfish, pipefish . . ."

". . . needlefish, jackfish, billfish, goldfish, spearfish, lungfish, swordfish, sunfish, starfish, moonfish, kingfish, queenfish, jellyfish, bonefish, and rockfish . . . but never a pumpkinfish! I should get a good price."

At the fish market, Otho was put on display with the other unusual seafood.

Otho's mother happened to be shopping for seafood that morning when . . . "Otho!" she cried. "Oh, my little Otho, we thought we'd lost you forever!" And then, after some spirited dickering, she bought Otho's head and a half-pound of mackerel.

When they got home, Otho was reunited with his body (his parents had kept it safe in a cool, dry place), and Otho's mother sat him on her knee. At first she smiled, and then her face grew serious. "You must be more careful, Otho," she said. "You know the world will always be difficult for a boy with a pumpkin for a head."

And Otho found that
suited him just fine.

For Bob Erickson

The images in *Pumpkinhead* are
multiple-color relief prints,
made on a Conrad E15 etching press
at Bob and Susan's farm
in Amherst Junction, Wisconsin.

THIS IS A BORZOI BOOK PUBLISHED BY ALFRED A. KNOPF

Copyright © 2003 by Eric Rohmann
All rights reserved under International and
Pan-American Copyright Conventions.
Published in the United States by Alfred A. Knopf,
an imprint of Random House Children's Books,
a division of Random House, Inc., New York,
and simultaneously in Canada by Random House
of Canada Limited, Toronto.
Distributed by Random House, Inc., New York.
KNOPF, BORZOI BOOKS, and the colophon are registered
trademarks of Random House, Inc.

www.randomhouse.com/kids

ISBN: 0-375-82416-2 (trade)
0-375-92416-7 (lib. bdg.)
Manufactured in China
10 9 8 7 6 5 4 3 2
August 2003
First edition